PLACERITA

Cover Artist: Lynne Hansen
Interior Design © 2023 by Brady Moller

ISBN: 978-1-58767-949-0

This book is a work of fiction. Names, characters, places and incidents either are products of the author's imagination or are used fictitiously. Any resemblance to actual events or locales or persons, living or dead, is entirely coincidental.

Cemetery Dance Publications
132B Industry Lane, Unit #7
Forest Hill, MD 21050

www.cemeterydance.com

PLACERITA

LISA MORTON
&
JOHN PALISANO

PLACERITA

I t was two minutes past midnight on March 13, 1928, when the power flickered and then went out in Alexis Crawford's cramped little college office. She looked up from the stack of biology papers she was grading, annoyed. All she could see was moonlight glinting on the odd gold figurine one of her students had given her. It was a curious piece, obviously antiquated, showing a squat human figure with the features of a lizard. Her student was more interested in the value of the gold than the folklore behind the piece, so she'd promised to return it when she was done researching it.

Something about it unnerved her now; or maybe it was being alone on the campus, late, in the dark. The University of California at Placerita was isolated, in the hills north of the sprawling San Fernando Valley, where it overlooked orange groves and barren chaparral. She inwardly cursed the school's wiring; she should have just taken the papers home. No, she'd chosen to stay here, but she was ready to go home now. She locked the fist-sized statuette in the bottom drawer of her desk, already thinking about lounging in her dad's favorite armchair, the one with the bright colors and worn wooden arms, cozy beneath a quilt her mother had made, sipping tea, warm, comfortable.

In an hour, Alexis would find that she no longer had a home.

WHEN THEY OPENED THE NEWHALL/VALENCIA AREA TO TRAFFIC AGAIN two days later, Alexis drove as close to the family ranch as she could, then she parked her Ford and got out to walk.

The power flicker she'd been irritated by had been the result of the collapse of the St. Francis Dam. The massive concrete structure had shattered like an eggshell beneath a giant's boot, sending a two-mile-wide, 140-feet high wave of destruction rushing across Southern California. God's wet hand simply erased canyon floors and hills, taking land and lives.

In Alexis's case, they were the same thing.

Her parents had died in the pneumonia outbreak of 1924, her father first, her mother two weeks later. An only child who'd left home three years earlier for graduate school, she'd been left with nothing but the ranch she'd grown up on. Located an hour north of Los Angeles, the ranch had once encompassed twenty acres of orchards and livestock pens, but when she'd lost her parents Alexis had sent away the laborers and let the business part of the ranch die with the citrus trees. She'd considered selling it all off, moving closer to L.A. proper, but she loved the old house, with its hacienda style and heavy furniture, the china that had been in her father's family for generations, the baskets she and her mother had made together. It all kept her connected to the family she still loved.

Now it was all gone forever.

Only a part of the main house's foundation was left, and even that was mostly covered up by debris the flood had brought from upstream. She stumbled across the rocky silt, uncaring that her feet sank in mud, looking for anything familiar, anything salvageable. Alexis felt numb, unreal. How could this mess of mud and rough stone be her home?

She paused in what she thought had probably been the main room of the house – the living room where her father's old favorite chair had rested less than forty-eight hours ago – and idly pushed silt around with one boot.

It hit her at once, a rush of emotion as hard and undeniable as the wave that had just rendered her life down to a flat wash of rubble. Alexis fell to her knees, her skirt pushed down into the dirt; she let the tears come, silent and hot.

When it passed, she found herself kneeling in the chaos, her knees beginning to hurt. She reached down to push herself up from the ground, and her hand fell on something oddly shaped buried just under the surface. It felt pliable, organic. Intrigued, she pulled it forth from ground that seemed reluctant to release it.

The object was obscured by a thick layer of muck; Alexis used her fingers to try to wipe it off. The more she revealed of what she'd found, the more astonished she was by it.

At first she thought – with so much revulsion that she briefly dropped the object and then had to force down her disgust to retrieve it – that what she'd found was a human hand. But as more of it came to light, she saw it was a hand, severed at the wrist, but scaled, the spaces between the fingers webbed. It was grayish-brown in color, sporting long, thick claws instead of nails at the end of each digit.

My God, could this be real?

Alexis was a biologist; confronted with this extraordinary piece, her training and scientific interest took over. She gently moved the fingers, touched the claws, examined the bone and sinew visible at the wrist. *The epidermal layer bends like I'd expect tissue to do. The bones look*

7

right. Seems to have real marrow and vessels inside. The skin looks authentic. Not dyed or synthetic. It looks like a real limb, not something bundled together.

Where did this come from?

The floodwaters had gushed over ten miles of Southern California arroyos and hillsides before they'd reached this point. Alexis had seen caves dotting some of those hillsides, had even heard rumors that some of them led down to deep tunnels full of gold left centuries ago by a race of...

Lizard people.

WHEN SHE FIRST MADE HER WAY DOWN THE HILL, SOLEDAD VILLAGE looked much like she'd remembered it. The steeple from St. Anne's stood high. The three lines of houses and streets that made up the main road still fanned out, and she remembered her father saying, "That's about the biggest fork you're ever going to see," as her mother sat quietly beside him in their truck, rolling her dark eyes at his bad jokes. But when Alexis drove closer she saw the drifts of mud leveling up, inside doorways and windows.

It looks like snow, if snow was made of sand.

She smelled the mineral-rich scent of water, still so prevalent. It was an alien smell so far inland. Soledad Village always smelled like the desert: hot, baking sand. Maybe the aroma of cooking once in a while. That was about it. But it never smelled wet. Not until after the dam broke.

Near the bottom of Canyon Road, she could turn left and travel southeast, toward Los Angeles and its outer towns. She wanted to turn right, drive down the main strip of Soledad Village, but a mound of sandy soil blocked the road. She stopped the car, pulling the handbrake. Her hands were still dirty from the mud and sand up at her decimated house. Even the seat was covered, her dress chaffing her shins. *Well, I'm already messed up. What's another trudge through the mud?* She stopped the engine and then turned around. *The hand is back there. Protect it.* Before she did, Alexis looked out to see if anyone was close. She saw no one, so she reached back, grabbed the specimen, wrapped it in a piece of curtain she plucked from a debris pile, and placed it gently on the back floor. *Maybe later tonight I can bring this back to the college and lock it up. Then come back tomorrow.*

But there were places she wanted – *needed* – to explore in the old town. She'd grown up there; it was a part of her. It was where her parents had met, when her mother had been running a little shop that sold native Gabrielino pottery and baskets, and her father had come to purchase feed for his livestock; later on, Alexis had gone to school and church there. She'd seen Mr. Alvarado, who ran the general store, just last month; he'd complained about his gout, told her how much he missed her parents, how she was pretty just like her mother. She'd hoped the village had been spared, but it was a mass grave now, silt and wreckage mounded around empty buildings. She wondered if folks had a chance to get out. *Are they still here? Buried in the mud? Have they gotten the bodies out yet? Will they even bother?*

She wasn't entirely sure if there'd been any official recovery efforts at Soledad Village. She could only assume there hadn't been. *Maybe something initially. Something basic. Nothing comprehensive.* Right now it was eerily empty, leaving Alexis to assume that any survivors had fled.

Survivors...there'd been so many people here she knew. Mr. Alvarado. Her school teacher, Mrs. Wood. Pastor Jenkins. They might all be dead.

She stepped from the car and shut the door. Turning her head to one side, she sighed. *You're a scientist. Distance yourself from this. Just get the facts. Look for any evidence.* She toed at a lump in the mud and found a child's metal pail, bright colors still visible behind the brown muck.

What if there's more here than toys and mud? If there was anything else like that hand...other pieces would have been washed down. Surely some would have been caught here before being pulled onward, forced up against walls or caught on foundations.

She knew she should return to the college, to the guest room in her Aunt Hazel's house in Providencia. She had so much to do. She had to rebuild her life. There would be insurance claims to deal with, papers to file, offices to visit. She couldn't stay with her aunt forever (and wasn't even sure she could stand another day), so she needed to find a new place to live. The work was daunting.

Alexis wasn't ready to face it yet. No, she could spare a few hours here, in a place she'd once loved, to pick through rubble looking for a miracle.

The mound looked almost as high as the car, which didn't bother her so much. At least no one would be able to see her easily from the road. *They'll know I'm here, though. The car gives it away. What if someone chances by? A policeman? Will they think I'm looting? What if they wonder what's in the backseat?*

Her mind turned to practicality, as it usually did. *How am I going to search? With my bare hands? Wouldn't it be better to have at least a shovel? And what am I going to wrap and gather any specimens with? Do I have anything in the car?*

She figured she'd first search the town for supplies. Her thoughts went to the different places inside the town. The General Store should have what she needed. Even if it'd been badly damaged, shovels and buckets would have been dirty, but intact and useable with very little effort. That was her plan.

Looking up at the mound, she sighed and said out loud, "Well, this is going to get messy."

"What is?" A voice said from behind her. How could there have been anyone there? She'd checked, after all.

When she turned, she recognized the speaker. He was a tall man with a drooping mustache, a spotless suit and hat, and fierce, furrowed brows. He was staring at her with an intensity that made her want to squirm like an ant beneath a magnifying glass. She'd seen his picture in the papers many times, most recently this morning.

William Mulholland. The chief engineer behind the construction of the St. Francis Dam and the last man to inspect it before it failed. Thousands were already calling for his head on a platter.

Why is he out here? Shouldn't he be talking to the press, or even to grieving widows?

Two other men walked up to join Mulholland. They were young, undistinguished looking, big. Even Alexis, who had no experience with crime outside of the picture shows, recognized them instantly as armed guards.

"I…uh…" Alexis stammered, gesturing vaguely behind her.

Mulholland said, "Speak up, girl!"

"I grew up here, in Soledad Village. I wanted to see if anything was left."

"Nothing." For an instant, Alexis thought she saw a flicker of regret cross Mulholland's features, but it was replaced immediately by steely resolve. "The flood destroyed it all. It's not safe around here, especially not for a young lady alone."

"Sir, I happen to be a professor of biology –" Alexis snapped her mouth shut, cursing her choice of words.

Too late – Mulholland had noticed. "Biology, you say? Have you come across anything…*odd?*"

Heart pounding, Alexis replied, "No. Why?"

Did they know? Had they seen her twitch, had she given the lie away? Were the two thugs about to step forward, pull guns from their coats and order her to empty her car?

And then it occurred to her: *How much does he know? Why did he ask me that?*

Mulholland squinted at her for what felt like an eternity before he offered a half-smile, indicating the interview – *interrogation?* – was over. "No reason. Good day, miss – I strongly urge you to get back in your car and go home."

Mulholland turned and began to walk away, but the two hired men stayed put. It was clear that they intended to wait until she was in her car and driving away.

Instead, she called out, "Mr. Mulholland…"

He tensed at hearing his name and then turned, slowly, to look at her.

"I don't have a home any more. My family's estate is gone now, wiped out by the flood."

Again, she thought she saw regret. "I'm truly sorry, Miss. But you don't want to have an accident in some sink hole created by the mud out here, go missing like that boy in the news…"

Walter Collins. He was a nine-year-old kid who'd been in all the papers for the last three days. His mother, Christine, had given him money and sent him off to the movies on the 10th, and he hadn't been heard from since. Theories ranged from the kid accidentally drowning in Lincoln Park Lake to a vindictive con out to settle a grudge with Walter's dad, who was currently doing time, to a link of some sort to a Mexican boy who'd been found dead in La Puente in February.

Why would Mulholland bring that up? Was it a threat? "Walter Collins…why would you -"

Mulholland cut her off. "Yes, yes, that's the one. Well, I'm sure the Los Angeles Department of Water and Power will offer you a generous settlement for your loss."

He strode off. Alexis watched him go, and only now noticed that there seemed to be someone sitting in the back seat of Mulholland's large, expensive car, someone with a wide-brimmed hat pulled down low over their eyes…someone who evidently didn't want to be recognized. *Who*, she wondered, *could be more worried about being spotted right now than William Mulholland?* As Mulholland climbed into his car and started it up, Alexis noticed that he inclined his head as if listening to something the rear passenger had said.

After a beat, Alexis reluctantly returned to her Ford, climbed in, made a U-turn, and drove past the thugs, who waited until she was well underway before joining Mulholland in his car.

At least she still had the hand.

WHEN ALEXIS REACHED HER AUNT HAZEL'S HOME, SHE WAS GLAD TO see that she was alone in the house; it was still mid-afternoon, and her aunt hadn't returned from her job as a bank teller yet. She'd left the hand, wrapped in several layers of paper and towels, in an icebox at the school, where she planned on examining it more thoroughly, and where she thought it was probably safest.

She showered and dressed, then sighed as she looked around the guest bedroom, its walls hung with crosses and framed art depicting Biblical scenes. She knew Aunt Hazel had a good heart - as soon as Alexis had called her at two in the morning after the dam disaster, her aunt had told her to come and stay with her, and they'd cried together on the living room couch. But Hazel was also obsessed with religion, and had often asked her niece if she actually believed "that nonsense that Mr. Darwin spouted about how we all came from monkeys and not the Good Lord and Adam's rib." Alexis had tried to explain to her aunt how evolution actually worked, but the woman couldn't seem to get over her notion that "our great grandparents were swinging from trees." Alexis's father used to say that his sister's religion had driven her husband, Tim, away. Alexis barely remembered Uncle Tim, who'd left his wife and headed back east somewhere a week after Prohibition went into effect. "He couldn't take all that god-fearing without a good, stiff belt," Dad would say, while Alexis's mother sat in her chair by the fire, working on a basket or embroidery, trying not to laugh.

Alexis noticed something new on a side table in the living room: it seemed to be a shrine to the evangelist Aimee Semple McPherson. Hazel had talked to her a few times about how powerful she thought McPherson was, and she'd urged Alexis to accompany her to see "Sister Aimee" preach in person. So far Alexis had evaded her Aunt's requests, but as she stood gazing down at the clutter of framed photos of the charismatic evangelist nestled in among Bibles and programs, she knew she'd have to agree. Besides, she was curious about Angelus Temple, the huge structure created to house the thousands who came every week to hear McPherson's latest sermon.

Alexis telephoned her dean at the university, assured him she'd be back to work by tomorrow, and then she sat down in Aunt Hazel's living room to go over want ads in the *Herald-Examiner*. She couldn't stay with Hazel forever, but she also had no idea where else to go. She hoped to someday rebuild on the Crawford land, but she knew it would be months, maybe years before she could undertake that project. In the meantime, she needed something else; as a single woman she probably wouldn't be able to get a loan on another house, but she thought she could find a boarding house where she could stay for a while. After all, her best friend from college, Olive, now shared an old Victorian in Angelino Heights with four other women she called her "flapper team." Alexis hoped she could find something near the university, which sat at the northern end of the Valley surrounded by orange groves,

She circled a couple of ads that might be worth following up on - a boarding house in North Hollywood wanted a "clean, quiet, single lady," a small house was for rent near the San Fernando Mission - but finally had to stop when she felt simply overwhelmed by it all.

Hazel jabbered nonstop as she drove them to Angelus Temple.

It was Sunday morning, and the streets between Hazel's home in Providencia and Sister Aimee's temple in Echo Park were quiet, but Hazel certainly wasn't. She apparently knew *everything* about Aimee Semple McPherson. She knew about her early days as a preacher, touring the eastern seaboard in a battered car with her mother and young daughter, setting up tents and preaching the gospel. She told Alexis about Sister Aimee's arrival in California, about how the Lord Jesus himself had directed her right to the location of her temple. She went on about the Sister's amazing radio sermons, and about how she was even more amazing in person at her temple, where she often staged elaborate theatrical performances as backdrops to her preaching.

Alexis had to admit that McPherson was intriguing; after all, *everyone* in Los Angeles had been obsessed with the woman two years ago, when she'd mysteriously disappeared while swimming in the ocean, only to turn up a month later with a kidnapping story that some people thought didn't quite hold water. "Aunt Hazel," Alexis said, secretly relishing the chance to needle her aunt a little, "didn't some reporter find out that she'd actually been holed up for a month in an adobe down in Mexico with a secret boyfriend?"

Hazel laughed before answering, "Oh, balderdash – you know that theory didn't stand up in the courtroom. Sister Aimee was *kidnapped*, and that's all there is to it."

Not long after that, the huge round structure that was Angelus Temple loomed before them. Hazel found a street parking space, pulled in, checked her hat and make-up in the car's mirror before stepping out, and Alexis followed. They soon joined a line of true believers waiting to enter the Temple, and Alexis found herself listening in on the conversations around them, which mainly centered on Sister Aimee's sermons or dresses or daughter or husband or her work converting sinners in speakeasys.

Finally they were admitted into the vast temple and seated near the back. Hazel had told her niece that the Temple seated 5,300, and looking around Alexis saw that was no exaggeration.

When Sister Aimee finally took the stage, wearing a nearly iridescent white dress, stepping up to a podium with multiple microphones, an awed hush fell over the crowd.

Whatever subject Alexis had expected to hear – maybe the virtues of charity, or a Biblical lesson on Jesus and the money-lenders – she was completely taken aback when McPherson launched into a fire-and-brimstone oratory about the evil forces surrounding them every day. The words, however, were nothing compared to the pageant that began to unfold behind the preacher, a visual presentation that

Alexis realized McPherson's millions of radio listeners would miss completely.

As the good Sister continued, speaking with passion that had her waving fists, behind her actors dressed in devil costumes cavorted on stage. A man wearing a red cape and an oversized papier mache mask painted bright red and sporting horns approached an older man in a business suit, thrusting a contract into his hands. On another part of the spacious stage, a demon offered a bottle of liquor to a young man, who took it and tilted it up, guzzling the contents. Another tempter held a beautiful but obviously skimpy dress out to a girl wearing rags; she raised her hands to her face in an outsized gesture of joy and happily accepted the satin garb.

Behind them all capered a costumed creature covered in shimmering brown-green scales; its head was low, elongated, flat, with a broad mouth and large, liquid eyes. Although it was hard to see details this far from the dais, Alexis thought the hands were clawed and webbed.

Her breath caught in her throat.

She fixed her gaze completely on that figure, tuning out Sister Aimee's fine words about fallen angels and temptation and how Jesus could save them. She watched as that figure ambled about the stage, moving slowly, heavily, while the other actors made extravagant gestures like overly-enthusiastic actors in regional theater productions.

Alexis ran through her Bible teachings in her mind, wondering if the scaled demon represented Satan when he took the form of a serpent in the Garden of Eden and brought about the fall of mankind; however, this thing, while reptilian, seemed definitely less like a snake than a lizard. Who had designed it and made the costume? How could it possibly tie in to what she'd found yesterday in the ruins of her home?

When Sister Aimee finally finished her sermon and the players left the stage, Alexis wanted to leap up, run after them, see where they went, where they stored the costumes. She'd love to examine that one up close, ask if anyone knew more about it.

Instead, she dutifully stood with the others to sing hymns, she contributed a few coins to the collections plates, and she watched the line form when Sister Aimee called those with ailments to come forward and be healed.

The queue of those waiting to be healed by Sister was long, and after twenty minutes of watching the preacher pray with them and tilt her head back to ask the Lord for blessings while paralyzed men shook and staggering women threw away their canes, Alexis asked if they could go. Hazel reluctantly agreed, but she was buoyant as they made their way out, glowing as they fell in with a small river of others leaving the temple. Hazel couldn't stop talking about Sister's new hair style, and Sister's dress, and Sister's beautiful voice, and after a few minutes Alexis began to wonder if Aunt Hazel was more interested in religion or fashion.

As they moved slowly along, Alexis tried to take in the entire temple, wondering where the pageant performers changed costumes, but she was swept towards the front lobby with the crowd.

As they headed outside, at last breaking free of the tight confines of the temple, Alexis cut her aunt off to ask, "What did you think of that bit with the demons tempting people right behind her?"

Hazel affectionately clapped Alexis on the shoulder. "Oh, I guessed you'd like that part; you always did prefer the fairy tales that had ogres in them."

"What about the costumes? I thought the one that looked like a reptile was particularly good."

Hazel's brow furrowed as she tried to recall. "Huh…can't say I noticed that one."

As they reached the car and started the drive back home, Aunt Hazel resumed her glowing review of Sister Aimee, but Alexis wasn't listening; her mind was preoccupied trying to find connections.

THAT NIGHT, ALEXIS WAS ALONE IN AUNT HAZEL'S KITCHEN (AUNT Hazel having bid her good night at the ripe old hour of 9 o'clock), poking through the icebox in search of a snack when she heard a knock at the front door.

Since her Aunt was already in bed (and asleep like a dead person – even Hazel joked that she could sleep through a hurricane), Alexis went to the front door, wondering who could be knocking this late on a Sunday night. She opened it, expecting to see a neighbor…

It was a big man in a suit with a broken nose and scarred chin visible beneath his broad hat. It took her a few seconds to place him: he was one of the men who'd accompanied Mulholland.

Her heart in her throat, she said, "Yes?"

The thug cleared his throat before saying, "Miss Crawford – I believe you know my employer, Mr. William Mulholland."

Alexis knew there was no point in playing dumb, so she answered, "I don't really know him – I've met him once, yesterday. You were there."

The man smirked slightly. "Good. That should make this easier, then."

"Make what easier?"

The man deliberately moved one leather-clad foot past the door frame and into Hazel's house, but made no move to enter. "Mr. Mulholland has reason to believe that you have something that doesn't belong to you."

Alexis's heart moved out of her throat back to her chest, where it began to hammer. "I don't know what you're talking about," she said, hoping she didn't sound as afraid as she felt.

"Look, girlie," the man said, leaning in, causing Alexis to involuntarily draw back, "something was found in the mud of that property that belongs to you, but that something was missing a piece, an *important* piece. We figure you might have that piece."

"Wait – you were rummaging around on *my* property? That's trespassing, Mister…"

"My name don't matter. What does is that you return what you found. We can do it the easy way and you can just give it to us, or we can do it the hard way and tear this joint up until we find it." The thug looked around Hazel's house, the threat clear.

"It isn't here," Alexis blurted out. "It's someplace safe, not nearby…"

Moving his eyes down to her, the man smiled and Alexis saw he had a gold front tooth. "Smart girl. Okay, you've got twenty-four hours." He pulled a card from his pocket and handed it to her. It had nothing but a phone number printed on it. "Call that when you've got it. We'll come and collect it, then you'll never see my ugly mug again. Sound fair?"

Alexis nodded. "Yes."

"Good," He started to turn away, but added, his voice lower, "Twenty-four hours. No more."

"I understand."

He tipped his hat, said, "Good night, Miss Crawford," and turned to leave.

Alexis immediately slammed the front door and locked it, then went to the front window, pulling back the curtains just an inch so she could look out. The man was walking back to a car parked at the curb; Alexis thought it was the same car she'd seen yesterday. As she watched, the darkness in the back seat of the car was punctuated by two yellow lights.

Eyes. The two lights were a pair of glowing eyes, looking back in her direction, unblinking. The car started up and pulled away, heading off down the street.

Alexis let out a long-held breath, allowed herself to collapse onto the couch, and thought about what her next step would be.

"WHATCHA GOT THERE, ALEXIS?"

Of everything Alexis had been through in the week since the flood – losing her home, finding the strange hand, the encounter with Mulholland, the creature onstage with Sister Aimee, the threatening encounter with the thug and what she'd glimpsed behind him – nothing had made her tense up quite like hearing Shufelt behind her. The fact that she hadn't noticed him coming into the lab didn't help any.

She'd never liked G. Warren Shufelt, who taught Engineering at Placerita. He was young, just a year or two older than Alexis, but full of fanciful notions rather than practical dreams. Alexis found some of Shufelt's ideas *so* fanciful that she occasionally wondered just how thoroughly his credentials had been checked before the university had hired him. The last time she'd talked to him, he'd told her about a device he was working on that he claimed could find objects through solid rock by using radio waves. Alexis was no engineering expert, but she thought Shufelt's invention sounded about as likely as a winged pig.

Of course, she was poking at what looked for all the world like a hand from a man-sized lizard.

After her late-Sunday-night visit, she'd decided to come to the university early and conduct as thorough an examination as she could before calling the number on the card. She'd already taken some small tissue slices and examined them under a microscope, figuring she could at least keep those since the missing bits would be unnoticeable given the amount of damage the hand had suffered in the flood. Even though it was starting to decay (she'd done her best to keep it on ice), it yielded fascinating results. It was plainly covered in a reptile's scales, not a mammal's skin; it was cold-blooded, a relatively young creature, powerful. She'd conducted her researches in secret; classes wouldn't start for another hour, and the campus was mostly empty at this hour. When she heard Shufelt behind her, she dropped the scalpel she'd been about to use to cut open part of the hand and dropped a towel over it.

"Just something for a class. Can I help you with something, Professor Shufelt?" She emphasized "Professor," hoping he'd get the point and stop calling her "Alexis," but in that respect, he seemed to be a perfectly typical male.

"It looked like a hand."

She turned, feeling her anger rising. Shufelt stood just inside the lab door, his head still craned to one side. "Were you spying on me?"

Shufelt shook his head, smiling. "No, of course not. It's just that…well…"

Of course he was spying on her. It made Alexis's skin crawl to think that it probably wasn't the first time.

"Mind if I take a look?" Before she could react, Shufelt crossed the room and yanked the towel aside.

He sucked his breath in before murmuring, "What have we here?"

Alexis inwardly sighed as she walked up to join him. "That's what I was trying to find out."

And then Shufelt said the one thing that could have surprised her. "I've seen one of these before."

Alexis stared in disbelief. "Where?"

"Have you ever heard of The Divine Order of the Royal Arm of the Great Eleven?"

Barely restraining a laugh, Alexis answered, "No."

"I know how that sounds, but the woman who runs it – Mrs. Blackburn – is aces. She's got a lot of strange things that believers have given her."

"'Believers'?"

"She lives not far from here, just above Santa Clarita. A hundred feet lower, and the flood would've wiped her out, too. She thinks the angels look after her."

"Shufelt…" Alexis was too irritated by his presence to bother with his title any longer. "I don't –"

"She's got a hand just like this. And I think a foot, too."

Alexis froze. After a few seconds, she said, "You've seen these things?"

He nodded and looked at her, smiling. "Sure. Do you want to see, too?"

Against her better judgment, Alexis nodded.

"I'll see what I can set up," Shufelt said, before winking at her.

Alexis felt her skin crawl as he left.

An hour later, she'd finished with the hand, ending her work by photographing it extensively. She called the number on the card, gave the address of the campus to the man who answered, and then waited in her office. Her first class started in two hours. She assumed they'd arrive before that.

The man she'd talked to last night was there in thirty-five minutes. He stood in the doorway to her office, looking around as if being in a place dedicated to learning made him nervous. "Whattaya got for me?"

Alexis handed him a bundle of towels. He pulled them away carefully, examined the hand briefly, sniffed it, and finally re-wrapped it. "Good. I'm sure I don't have to tell you to keep your trap shut about this. If this were to show up in the local papers…" He let the rest of the sentence hang in the air like a suspended blade.

"It won't," Alexis assured him.

"Make sure it don't." With that he was gone, leaving Alexis to breathe a little easier and hoping she'd never see him again.

Two days later, Alexis found a boarding house in the sleepy valley town of Burbank. Her travel to and from work would be short, and the boarding house was run by a friendly middle-aged woman named Victoria who welcomed Alexis with only a few requirements, chiefly that she actually pay her rent every week.

The house, a lovely old gingerbread with three floors, had six boarders including Alexis, all currently female ("Cuts down on the hanky-panky," Victoria had said with a broad smile). Alexis's nearest neighbor was a pretty young girl trying to become an actress; she told Alexis her birth name (because her mother had been a cousin of one of Los Angeles's founding families) had been Graciela de Feliz, but that name would never fly in Hollywood so she went by Grace Henry (she'd chosen the last name because she hoped it sounded like royalty). She was bubbly and sweet-natured, and decided instantly that Alexis was going to be her new best friend, despite their differences in age, temperament, and profession.

When Alexis had packed up her single bag, Aunt Helen had of course hugged her and told her she could stay, but Alexis thought her Aunt was also secretly glad to get her quiet home back. Thankfully, Helen had slept through the episode with Alexis's late-night visitor, but Alexis knew there were other reasons she couldn't stay much longer with Helen, who she suspected would soon be applying more pressure to convert.

Grace helped Alexis set up her room, and listened as Alexis told her about losing the family home in the St. Francis Dam disaster. "Oh, honey, that's terrible. Well, I'm glad you landed here." Grace peered at her new friend for an instant, and then said, "You need something to cheer you up. What are you doing tonight?"

"Uhhh...nothing."

With a sly smile, Grace said, "I got to be an extra today in a scene shot by Mr. D. W. Griffith himself – I mean, I'm just in a crowd scene with a thousand other folks, but it was still an honor to watch him work – and I met an assistant director who told me how to get into Club Intime – wanna go?"

Alexis stared blankly, trying to take it all in. "What is Club Intime?"

Grace made a comical face of mock disbelief as she answered, "Oh, Ally, we need to broaden your horizons! It's the hottest speakeasy in town; I mean, that's what I've heard. I haven't actually been there yet. It's owned by Texas Guinan and it sounds like so much fun!"

"A speakeasy? You mean, where they drink?"

"Drink, and dance…" Grace did an exaggerated Charleston that made Alexis laugh, then she stopped and looked at Alexis. "Say you'll go. It'll just be the two of us, out on the town for a night of thrills and luxury."

Alexis surprised herself by saying, "I'll go."

Grace clapped her hands in excitement. "You're the bee's knees! Be ready about nine?"

"Okay."

Grace left the room and Alexis sat on the bed, wondering what on earth she'd just agreed to.

It was nine-thirty when the two women walked up to a big man who stood in an alley next to stairs leading down to a basement door. For an instant Alexis had a jolt of fear – was he her unnamed thug? – but then she saw this man had a mop of black hair poking out from beneath his fedora and no facial scars, and she relaxed.

Grace strode up to the man, said, "I'm here to see Tex," and the man grunted and nodded down the stairs. At the bottom of the steep flight, Grace knocked on a metal door. A small panel inset in the door slid aside and another man looked out. Grace repeated the phrase and the door opened.

Even though they were at the end of a long hallway, the sound was already loud: live music, whoops and hollers. Grace was chattering excitedly about celebrities who were said to frequent the club, but Alexis didn't recognize most of the names.

They turned a corner, passed through an open doorway – and entered another world.

Club Intime was a huge basement space, part of a secret network of tunnels and rooms that ran beneath the streets of L.A.; Grace had told Alexis that many of the tunnels had originally been built by the Chinese, who used them back in the 1800s to hide from angry white mobs, but that some of the underground passages were even older and no one knew exactly who'd built them. Club Intime had a stage and dance floor at one end, bars on either side of the room, and the rest of the floor taken up with tables and chairs. The space was packed, the dance floor bouncing, a twenty-piece band onstage playing fast jazz while a chorus line of eight costumed girls kicked and shimmied before them. Alexis – who would've been the first to admit that she'd led a sheltered life, mainly in the placid hills at the north end of the San Fernando Valley – had never seen anything like it, and she spent a few seconds staring in wonder before she realized that Grace was pulling her along. "C'mon, I see an empty table!"

They grabbed two chairs and were just seated when the song came to an end, and applause exploded as a beautiful woman in her mid-forties stepped onto the stage. She grabbed a microphone and shouted, "Hello, suckers!" The applause that greeted her was deafening.

"Who's that?" Alexis asked, leaning in to Grace so she could be heard.

"That's Texas Guinan herself!" Grace leaned back to clap with everyone else.

A man at a table near the front shouted, "I love you, Tex!"

Guinan looked down from the stage and responded, "I love you, too – depending on what's in your wallet!"

The crowd burst into laughter, and Alexis couldn't help but join in. A waiter approached, and Grace ordered whiskey. The drinks arrived a few minutes later; even though it was homemade hooch that burned her throat going down, Alexis sank into the way it relaxed her.

The two friends drank and laughed for a while; then a man approached the table and asked Grace to dance. She gave Alexis a look of faux surprise, and Alexis waved her off. As they moved to join the dancers, Alexis heard a small commotion happening near the entrance, turned to look...and gaped in shock when she saw Aimee Semple McPherson just entering.

She remembered, though, that Aunt Helen had told her that Sister Aimee sometimes visited speakeasies for no other reason than to bring these wayward sheep back to the Lord, and sure enough, the preacher was moving among the crowd with a small entourage, handing out flyers, doling out dazzling smiles, clad in a shimmering white dress that made it seem as if she floated through the decadence in a state of unassailable purity.

"Well, now," Texas shouted into the mic, "I see Sister Aimee's arrived so the next round is on her!" The place exploded in hilarity and approval.

Grace leaned in to Alexis and said, "Too bad your Aunt's not here."

Alexis responded, "I don't think she'd want to see her idol in this setting."

Grace chuckled and took another sip of bad liquor.

Alexis spent a few seconds watching Sister Aimee work the room, marveling at how she sidestepped attempted pinches and never lost her composure. She glanced away at one point, and noticed something she hadn't seen before: to the side of one of the bars, a hallway receded into darkness, and a man stood just inside, looking out on the proceedings. He was clad in a long dark coat, had his hands in the pockets, his face hidden under a wide-brimmed hat – and eyes that shone with yellow luminescence.

Her heart skipping a beat, Alexis stared. The man – or *not* a man – was probably a hundred feet away, separated from her by a sea of revelers...and yet she swore that his gaze had just moved from following Sister Aimee to fix on *her*. Their eyes locked for a few seconds before he turned and disappeared down the unlit hallway.

Alexis was instantly on her feet, dimly aware that Grace was calling, "Where you going?" The whiskey had settled in and she fought to stay on feet as she worked her way through the crowded tables and around the edge of the gyrating dancers. Finally she reached the hallway and peered down its dimly lit length. It was short, with three closed doors spaced along it. The figure was nowhere in sight. Alexis tried each of the doors; one opened onto a kitchen, one revealed a small storage room, but the third was locked, with "NO ADMITTANCE" stenciled across it.

"Somethin' I can help you with, darlin'?"

Alexis started and spun to see Texas Guinan herself watching her from halfway down the hall, leaning casually against a wall. "Oh, I…" Alexis stammered, unable to produce even a lie.

"Let me tell you something, kid," Texas said, seriously, "you need to forget whatever you think you just saw. It's none of your business, and it'll get you killed or worse if you keep lookin' for it."

Alexis gulped like a nervous schoolgirl in the principal's office. "Yes, Miss Guinan."

"Now get back out there and enjoy yourself. You're too damned young not to."

As Alexis walked by her, Guinan said, in a hushed voice, "And for God's sakes, *stay out of the tunnels.*"

By the time Alexis returned to Grace, Sister Aimee had left, and she knew the night was over for her as well.

ALEXIS ONLY HAD TWO CLASSES TO TEACH THE FOLLOWING DAY, SO SHE decided to spend her afternoon visiting the new Central Public Library in downtown Los Angeles. Although it was already two years old, she hadn't been yet.

She left her car at the boarding home and took Red Car trains to the downtown area. The library was only a block away when she stepped down from the electric train car, and the building's imposing bulk and gracious design made it easy to spot.

Stepping inside gave her the sense of serenity she'd always found in libraries; surrounded by great works of literature and science and history always left her feeling both humbled and excited (to explore their wonders). This library, with its spacious overhead arches and artfully placed windows to allow in some natural lighting, delighted her and calmed the anxiety she'd felt since the flood.

She found the section on books of local history, but was uncertain where to begin – would any of them actually talk about a system of tunnels beneath Los Angeles? Alexis decided she'd better start by consulting an expert, so she strode up to the reference desk.

The librarian on duty was a man of about thirty, tall and slender, with thick brown hair, round spectacles, suspenders, and a bow tie; Alexis could imagine Grace calling him "cute as a June bug," and then urging her to ask him something provocative.

"Excuse me," she said, waiting until he looked up from something he was reading, "but I'm looking for something very specific about local history, and I'm hoping you can help me."

He smiled, and Alexis liked the effect. "Sure," he said, "tell me more and let's see what we can come up with."

"I'm looking for anything about tunnels running beneath Los Angeles."

The man's eyebrows shot up at that. "Oh," he said, and Alexis realized instantly she'd asked the right question of the right person. "Tunnels. I see. What kind of information are you looking for?"

"Well…" she had to think for a moment, because even she wasn't sure, "…I guess anything about their history – how far back they go, who might have originally built them, that kind of thing."

"You mean like lizard people?"

Alexis froze, staring in shock. After a few seconds, the young man smiled. "Don't worry, you're not the first one to ask about this, especially since the rumors got out about the library's basement."

"The…library's basement?"

"Yes...oh, you don't know about that?"

Alexis shook her head, her perplexity growing. "No, I don't. I was at a...well, someplace else last night and someone mentioned the tunnels to me, and I..."

"Ahh." The man looked around briefly, then said to Alexis, "Wait here – I'll be right back."

He disappeared for a few seconds before returning with a middle-aged woman. "Mrs. Dunleavy will watch the desk for a few minutes so I can show you something." He stepped out from behind the waist-high counter and waved her down between the stacks. "This way."

Intrigued, Alexis followed until he led them to a door marked STAFF ONLY. He used a key to unlock it, and beyond was a simple hallway with offices and storerooms along its length. After the door closed behind them, he turned to offer her a hand. "Oh, sorry, I should've introduced myself – I'm Ambrose Charles."

"Alexis Crawford." Alexis took his hand, and liked the way it felt: warm, dry, the grip firm without trying to crush. From his smile, she guessed he felt the same way. After several seconds longer than a handshake should've taken, they pulled apart and Alexis saw his face redden.

He opened another door at the end of the hallway to reveal a stairwell. They went down, descending to the bottom, where they stepped through a metal door into a dimly-lit corridor.

"There isn't much down here, except some storage rooms..." He walked to the far end of the hallway, which was lit only by low-wattage bulbs spaced far apart overhead. The final door was completely different from all the others they'd passed: it was metal, thick and heavy, and had no knob or handle.

"This is it," Ambrose said, stopping at the door. "A lot of people believe this door opens directly into the tunnel system that runs beneath L.A."

Alexis eyed the door before looking to Ambrose. "Have you been through it?"

"Can't. Look at it – no way to open it from here. It can only be opened from the *other* side."

"Why?"

Ambrose shrugged, then stepped closer to her, sending a delicious chill along Alexis's spine. "Some people say," he spoke softly, directly into her right ear, "that this door leads to a kingdom of lizard people who once lived beneath L.A. in tunnels lined with panels of pure gold."

Alexis turned to look at him, saw both amusement and sincerity there. "What do *you* think?"

Ambrose abruptly frowned. "I had to come down here once to retrieve a rare book I had a call for, and I…well, I swear I heard *scratching* on the other side of this door, like something with claws was trying to get in."

They both went silent then, ears straining…but, except for their breathing, there was only silence.

After a few seconds, Alexis surprised herself by saying, "Have you ever been to Texas Guinan's speakeasy? It's only a few blocks from here."

Ambrose reacted in faux surprise. "Speakeasy? Why, Miss Crawford, you aren't suggesting we *imbibe*, are you? I mean, that would be breaking the law."

He stepped closer; Alexis felt his heat, his nearness, and for a moment she thought he might kiss her…if she didn't kiss him first. "No, Mr. Charles," she said, smiling shyly, "I'm sure there are plenty of people who go there just to talk."

"Would you like to go talk there maybe, Friday night?"

Before she could answer, a BANG sounded on the other side of the locked door. They both broke off, staring, listening, as something that might have been a bolt being drawn back sounded. Ambrose grabbed her hand and pulled her away. "Let's go," he said, his voice shaking.

When they reached the far end of the hall, Alexis looked back a last time. She heard the door creaking open on ancient, seldom-used hinges, and saw the glint of yellow eyes. Then they were racing up the stairs and Ambrose had slammed the door to the stairwell.

Neither of them slowed down until they had returned to the reference desk, the calming presence of the books all around them. The salt-and-pepper-haired Mrs. Dunleavy looked up at them curiously. "You two look like you just saw a ghost," she said.

Alexis looked toward the door marked STAFF ONLY before answering, "A ghost would be preferable."

AMBROSE ENDED UP SUGGESTING A HISTORY OF CALIFORNIA MISSIONS TO Alexis, and as she read the book that night in her bed at the boarding house, she discovered why: one of the early friars who founded the missions mentioned a strange rumor among the Indians of "lizard people." There was nothing more, just that single mention.

Alexis noted the author of the book was a Franciscan monk named Zephyrin Engelhardt, and according to his biography at the rear of the book he now resided at the mission in Santa Barbara.

Alexis returned the book personally two days later, found Ambrose, was gratified to see his obvious pleasure in meeting her again, took a breath of courage, and asked if he'd like to drive to Santa Barbara with her on Saturday. He not only agreed, he offered to drive.

The trip took two hours, the roads winding through orange groves and green hills studded with California oaks and small towns where cowboys on dusty horses traipsed down Main Street. Better than the scenery, though, was the talk, as Alexis and Ambrose introduced themselves more thoroughly. Alexis spoke of growing up as a girl interested in a science, who as a teenager had wanted to research and investigate, but because of her gender had found those paths closed to her, so she'd become a teacher instead. She reminisced on what it was like growing up with a mother who was half-native Gabrielino, how her mother had nurtured a love of living things in her and protected her from the bullies she accrued whenever her heritage was discovered.

Ambrose revealed his own background as a young man whose love of books had subjected him to juvenile attacks; fortunately, he'd had an uncle who'd been a successful amateur boxer and had taught him to defend himself. His family had come to Los Angeles when he was ten (for his father's work as an architect), and he'd fallen in love with his new home instantly. By the time they reached Santa Barbara, he and Alexis had discovered that they shared a mutual affection for the works of the Bronte sisters, the music of Chopin, and the fiery orange California poppies that dotted the local hillsides each spring.

Once they arrived in Santa Barbara, a stop at a gas station provided directions for the final leg of the trip, and they soon pulled up before the gorgeous Mission Santa Barbara. It sat in the middle of fifteen acres of field and garden, with a few houses behind. The current church, with its white stone, red trim, double bell towers, and an arched colonnade stretching away to the left, was more than a century old. The air was scented by tart citrus from the nearby trees; a glance into the orchards revealed olives and sugar cane as well. They parked beside a stone fountain with lily pads floating on the surface, and walked through the open doors of the church itself.

Alexis hadn't expected to be met by Friar Engelhardt, who at 77 she assumed would no longer be serving in the church, and indeed a younger man welcomed them, and then asked them to wait in the rear of the church. They were both quiet as they sat, awed by the beauty of the church's interior, with its warm wood and ornate gold gleaming in candlelight.

A few moments later, the young Friar who'd greeted them returned with a surprisingly spry older man who also wore the brown cassock of the Franciscans and could only be Zepherin Engelhardt. He had a heavily lined and bearded face, thin but with kind and curious eyes.

Alexis had secretly been nervous about this whole trip; growing up, her mother had told her stories that she'd heard from her grandparents about how the Catholic missionaries had enslaved their people to build their missions. As a result, Alexis held a lifelong mistrust of priests and friars…but there was something about Engelhardt that put her at ease.

Alexis and Ambrose introduced themselves, and Alexis explained that they'd driven from Los Angeles because she'd just read his *Missions and Missionaries* and had some questions. He nodded, apologized for his age, and suggested they talk in his cell.

Englehardt's simple room had a cot, a standing wardrobe, and a desk that was cluttered with papers, books, and knickknacks. Alexis instantly noticed a small red seed pot with a sculpted lizard crawling around the side, except the lizard seemed to have human hands and feet; the similarity to the gold piece the student had shown her was striking. "What is this, Friar?" she asked as she bent close to peer at it.

"Ahh, yes, that is an interesting piece. It was a gift to me by an artist who came from local Gabrielino Indian stock, and it represents a legend of lizard people who once walked the land here."

Alexis and Ambrose exchanged a look, then Alexis asked, "That's actually what I wanted to ask you about: you mentioned this belief briefly in your book…"

"Yes. I once heard a legend of a race of lizard-men who lived in this area in buildings of gold, but when the Gabrielinos arrived the lizards took their gold and fled underground, where they fell into a kind of hibernation-sleep in their gold-lined tunnels. The Indians believed they would awaken again at the end of the world."

"Friar…" Alexis weighed her words carefully, "do you think there was any basis for those legends?"

The elderly friar smiled. "If you're asking me whether I believe in a race of lizard men…well, I could only say that the Gabrielinos – like all non-Christian primitives – live with many superstitions."

Alexis abruptly found the man's face less kindly, his knowledge less wise. This was a man who believed in demons and angels, but the beliefs of everyone else were superstitious? "My mother," she said, feeling her color rise, "was half-Gabrielino, and told me of how the missionaries enslaved the natives to build these churches…"

Engelhardt's smile didn't waiver as he responded, "The natives gladly accepted Christ and it was in their loving roles as acolytes that they built these temples to God."

Rising, Alexis got out a terse, "Thank you for your time, Friar," before marching out.

Ambrose followed but ran ahead of her to open the car door. "Did you get anything useful at all out of that?"

She paused before climbing into his car. "Yes. Mainly that my mother was right when she told me to stay away from religious men."

Ambrose got in behind the wheel, started the car, turned to her before pulling out. "Hey, I've got an idea: since we're here and it's a nice day, what do you say we take a walk on the beach?" When she was slow to respond, he added, "I can't guarantee that we'll meet any lizard men, but maybe we'll find a nice seashell or two."

Alexis had to smile at that. "That sounds lovely, Ambrose."

They drove a few blocks to the cliffs above the shore, where they continued until the road took them down to the beach front. They parked, had lunch at a diner, and then spent the afternoon walking in the sand, taking their shoes and socks off as water splashed around their feet. The sun was soon setting on the western horizon, painting the Pacific in deep blue with a radiant orange and indigo sky overhead. They paused to admire the beauty, Ambrose gently slipping his hand into Alexis's. She lightly squeezed his fingers, and he leaned in to kiss her, a soft touch that she returned. When they pulled apart, warmed even as the sun's heat vanished, Alexis knew something in her life had just changed, maybe forever.

The drive home was quiet, as Ambrose controlled the car mainly with one hand so he could hold Alexis's with the other. When he dropped her at the boarding house, they shared a quick brush of the lips, then she was waving as he drove off, as happy as she'd ever been despite the visit with Engelhardt.

Grace was inside the front door, waiting to greet her with a knowing smile. "Who was *that* driving away in the nice car?"

"His name is Ambrose Charles, he works at the new public library downtown, I met him on Thursday, and we just got back from Santa Barbara, where he kissed me on the beach." She turned and headed for her room, enjoying the stunned expression on her friend's face.

Tired from the day's events, Alexis crawled into bed early, hoping to dream of Ambrose. Instead, her sleep was disturbed by visions of darkness that held hissed whispers and indefinable dread. Glowing eyes glided here and there, peering at her but disappearing before she could follow them. Her cries for help were ignored, her fear increasing as she found no light, no comfort, no warmth.

She awoke in the night with the overwhelming sense that something terrible was about to happen.

ON MONDAY MORNING, ALEXIS FOUND TIME IN BETWEEN HER CLASSES to call the downtown library and ask for Ambrose Charles. She'd decided to be a truly modern woman and invite him to dinner.

The History Department librarian told her that Ambrose hadn't shown up for work that morning.

Alexis tried to ignore the dread that abruptly filled her, but the dreams of two nights ago had left her filled with foreboding. She realized that didn't even have Ambrose's home phone number or address, so all she could do was wait.

Her answer came with the Tuesday morning newspaper: there, buried in the local news section, was a story headlined "Downtown Librarian Dies in Freak Accident." The article said the body of Ambrose Charles, 28, who worked in the history department, had been found at the bottom of a flight of stairs leading to the library's basement, his neck broken.

The newspaper fell from Alexis's nerveless fingers, grief warring with guilt. Had Ambrose been killed because of her? That didn't make any sense; if someone – Mulholland, or the thing with glowing yellow eyes – had wanted to threaten her, why not just do it directly? Besides, she'd returned the hand, so weren't they finished?

No, she realized Ambrose had died for some other reason. She thought that perhaps he'd gone back down to the door to attempt to open it, seeking some sort of proof for her – and he'd gotten more proof than he'd bargained for. She guessed he hadn't really died of a broken neck, or at least not a broken neck that had happened in a *fall*.

No, he'd been murdered by something that didn't want to be found, at least not by him.

She was having breakfast with Grace and Victoria and the other boarders when she read the news, and Grace was the first to notice her expression. "Honey, what's wrong?"

Unable to answer, Alexis fled the table, ran up the stairs to her room, closed the door and began to sob. She cried for her part in Ambrose's death, for the end of his life, for the end of the life she might have had with him. When Grace came in to comfort her, she cried in her friend's arms; finally, in strangled gulps, she told Grace that Ambrose was dead.

"Oh my God! Oh, Ally, I'm so sorry."

An hour later, her tears spent, Alexis felt her grief replaced by anger and resolution. She'd be damned if she'd let Ambrose's death go unchallenged and uninvestigated. She'd find out what dreadful secret the City of Angels was built on, and she'd expose it to the world, Mulholland and his thugs be damned.

She thought about her next move, and decided it was time to take Shufelt up on his offer to introduce her to someone who had their own proof.

On the following Saturday, Shufelt drove Alexis to meet the woman who he claimed had a hand like the one Alexis had relinquished. She wasn't entirely comfortable with being in a car alone with Shufelt, but he spent the entire hour-long drive into the hills above the Valley talking nonstop about how Mrs. Blackburn had opened his eyes in a way that had boosted his creativity and soon his inventions would be utilized around the globe.

Alexis had never heard him speak at length about this before; finally she cut him off as he was praising Mrs. Blackburn's extraordinary skills in prediction and said, "Why, Warren, you sound like someone in a cult."

He shook his head a little too vigorously. "Oh, no, it's not like that! Cults are led by fakes, and Mrs. Blackburn is no fake. You only need to hear her talk for a few moments to realize that she's the real deal."

Alexis began to fear this whole trip had been a bad idea.

After leaving the main route that led west out of the Valley and towards the distant coastline, they turned north and bumped up a dirt road into a canyon. At one point they drove by a graveyard of rusted-out trucks and cars. "What's with all the wrecks?" Alexis asked.

"Oh, sometimes when the new folks arrive they offer up their cars as sacrifices."

Alexis thought, *Not a cult my foot*, but what she said was, "Sacrifices to who, exactly?"

Warren didn't answer.

Alexis tried to tell herself these people were just isolated eccentrics, but she increasingly wished she'd gone to Texas Guinan and tried to pump her for more instead. At least the bootlegger was more interested in cold, hard cash than sacrifices.

The trip ended before a sprawling, wooden ranch house surrounded by a dozen cabins and other outbuildings. A nervous young woman answered the door, obviously recognized Shufelt, and led them into a parlor where the owner of the house, May Otis Blackburn, waited. She was a middle-aged woman who had never been beautiful, but there was something sly about her features. She didn't rise to greet them, but remained seated at a small table, scrutinizing Alexis. Blackburn was sipping something clear from a glass, but judging from her expression it wasn't water.

Shufelt walked up to the woman and knelt before her until she tapped his shoulder. "You may rise, my son," she said. He did, backed away, and threw a hand out toward Alexis. "Mrs. Blackburn, this is the young woman I told you about, Alexis Crawford." When Shufelt looked back to Blackburn, his eyes shone with adoration. "And this is May Otis Blackburn, prophet of The Divine Order of the Royal Arm of the Great Eleven."

Alexis started to offer her hand, but caught herself – how was one supposed to greet a so-called prophet? She wasn't about to kneel as Shufelt had, but she also didn't think the woman was interested in touching her hand. She settled for, "I'm pleased to make your acquaintance, Mrs. Blackburn."

Just then they heard a knock on the front door. The nervous young woman answered, exchanged a few words with someone, and then stepped out of the house. Glancing through the front windows, Alexis saw her leading two ice delivery men who carried a huge block between tongs.

Shufelt saw it, too. "Is that for the priestess?"

Blackburn nodded. "We won't need that much longer, though. It's been almost twelve-hundred-and-sixty days; she'll be coming back soon."

Shufelt nodded, muttered, "Praise God."

"Now," Blackburn said, scrutinizing Alexis again, "let's talk about why you're here. Warren tells me you recently found something very curious that might interest me."

Alexis was increasingly reluctant to share her find with this woman, but since it was unlikely that she was anything but a charlatan there was probably nothing to lose. "I lost my home in the St. Francis Dam flood, and when I went to examine the ruins I found something that looked like a human hand, but covered in scales."

Blackburn took another sip from her drink before saying, "I see. And you're sure it was authentic?"

"Yes, quite sure. I examined it carefully in my lab —"

Cutting her off, Blackburn asked, "Your 'lab'?"

"Yes, at the University of California, Placerita. I teach biology there."

"You're a professor? You seem awfully young. Young, and . . ."

"A woman," Alexis said. "Yes, well, I graduated with my master's degree from UCLA four years ago, and UCP was in desperate need of biology teachers."

May tilted her drink towards Alexis in a toast, said, "Don't sell yourself short, dear. You've achieved remarkable things for one so young."

For a second Alexis warmed to Blackburn, who had just paid her a compliment she hungered for but seldom heard...and then she reminded herself: *This is what conmen do: tell people what they want to hear until they're ready to give anything to hear it again.*

"So, this specimen...do you have it with you?"

"No," Alexis answered. "But I have these." She reached into her purse to withdraw some of the photos she'd taken of the hand.

Blackburn glanced at them, set her glass down, rose from her chair and said. "My dear, please join me in my study. Warren, you stay here." She strode from the room, Alexis following.

Blackburn led them out of the parlor and down a short hallway to a study overflowing with boxes, files, and books. Even the desk looked as if it'd been last organized a decade earlier; there was a stack of hand-written pages on one corner, with a ream of blank sheets on the other. In the middle of the desk was a Holy Bible, a half-filled page, and a pen and ink.

Blackburn gestured to the pages. "As a professor, you've no doubt written a book or two..."

Smiling wanly, Alexis answered, "Not yet."

"Ahh," Blackburn said, with just the slightest hint of condescension. "I myself am in the middle of a work that I believe will rival Mr. Manly Hall's *The Secret Teachings of All Ages.* I call my book *The Great Sixth Seal*; it's a gathering of all the secrets conveyed to me by the Archangel Michael. I'm quite sure it will change the world when it's published."

"How interesting," Alexis said, forcing a smile.

Blackburn gestured to a pair of well-worn leather seats away from the desk, near a cluttered bookcase. "Sit. Sit," she said. "We have much to discuss."

Alexis sat, preparing herself for what she thought would surely be some attempt to convert her. Shufelt (and her other followers) might consider this woman to be a prophet, but Alexis saw her as something quite different. Maybe it was the practiced smile, which Alexis had seen so many times at street fairs and boardwalks.

"Now, let's take a look again at those pictures." Alexis passed the photos over, waiting as Blackburn examined them carefully.

"May I ask where the actual object is now?"

Alexis paused, considering the best way to frame her answer. "It was…returned to someone who claimed ownership of it."

May handed the photographs back, saying, "I'll bet it was. I may have the only specimens they haven't been able to steal back."

Alexis's eyes widened. "You have specimens? Here?"

"Oh yes, all carefully preserved."

"Is it possible to see them?"

May sat forward. "We both know that's why you're here. You're showing me yours and I'm showing you mine."

"Yes," Alexis said. "I'm just surprised they're here instead of in a climate-controlled facility."

"What do you think the ice was being brought in for?" Blackburn didn't rise yet, but took a pause to examine Alexis again. "My dear, may I ask what your religious beliefs are?"

Here we go, Alexis thought. "I'm not a religious person," she answered.

"You prefer science."

"Yes, I guess you could say that."

Blackburn nodded in the direction of the front parlor. "Warren was like that when he came to us. Sometimes skeptics make the best novitiates. Once your eyes are opened, you can't just close them again."

"I'm quite comfortable with my beliefs, Mrs. Blackburn."

Leaning closer, Blackburn asked, "Have you ever seen a miracle, Miss Crawford? A *real* miracle, something your science couldn't explain?"

"No."

"Would you change your mind if you did?"

Alexis shrugged. "Possibly, but…"

"What if, for example, you saw the creature that went with that hand?"

I think I already have, Alexis nearly said, but instead replied, "I'd adjust my science."

"Even if you saw *hundreds* of them?"

Alexis gaped for a second, stunned by the thought. "That's impossible…"

"What if I told you that they've been here all along, living right beneath us?"

"I'd say there's no proof of that."

Nodding at the photographs Alexis still held, Blackburn said, "But you've got the proof right there; you yourself said it was authentic."

"It's…that's…" Alexis as disturbed to find herself stammering, so she forced an answer. "It's probably just the result of mutation, an aberration in a single animal…"

Blackburn inhaled before saying, "They're very angry at Mulholland right now. In fact, they believe the flood was a deliberate attack. It killed hundreds of them."

"How would you know that?"

"The Archangel communicated it to me. And…well, I've had a visit from Mr. Mulholland."

Alexis thought back, wondering if she'd ever said anything to Shufelt about Mulholland, or let slip something to Blackburn that she'd correctly guessed indicated Mulholland's involvement. She couldn't remember anything like that. She asked simply, "When?"

"A year ago. You see, one of my followers had been engaged in some prospecting not far from here, and had come across something far more interesting than gold. They brought their findings to me, somehow Mulholland got wind of it, and he came here to see for himself."

"Did you show him your…'findings'?"

Blackburn shook her head. "No. In fact, I lied and told him I had nothing. There was something about Mr. Mulholland I didn't trust, so I sent him away." She paused before smiling at Alexis and adding, "But Michael tells me to trust you, my dear, so…would you like to see?"

Somewhat numb, Alexis answered, "Yes. I would."

Blackburn rose and gestured to a door on the other side of the study. "This way."

The door opened on a short hall that went to an exit at the rear of the building. Blackburn led the way across a dusty, barren yard full of broken tools and equipment, to an outbuilding that had no windows and a heavy steel door. She opened the door, and Alexis flinched as a blast of cold air hit her, then she remembered the blocks of ice she'd seen being brought in.

Blackburn kept the door open as she paused to light a lantern kept nearby, and then she closed it, sealing them in. Alexis shivered, as much from the thought of being trapped in a dark room with May Otis Blackburn as the cold. Blackburn took the lantern and swung it around the chamber. The blocks of ice were stacked in the center, while the sides held various containers. One long, low copper container had Alexis puzzled, until it occurred to her that it looked like…*a small casket,* child-sized.

Blackburn must have seen her expression. "That holds our priestess, Willa. The poor child was taken by God at the age of sixteen, but she will resurrect soon in the first of a series of promised miracles." She moved the light away from the casket over to a long metal shelf against one wall. "Over here."

Alexis joined her to see that the shelf held several large glass jars, objects floating in each one. Blackburn held the lantern close to the one in the middle, indicating where Alexis should look. Leaning in, Alexis saw something that did indeed bear a resemblance to her lizard hand. "It is similar, but —"

Blackburn cut in sharply, "It's *exactly* the same."

Leaning in closer, Alexis ran her eyes over the hand in the jar. The color was indeed close to the grayish-green of her hand, the size similar, the claws at the ends of the digits almost alike, but…there was a line running down one side. Alexis squinted, trying to see, but Blackburn shifted the lantern. "Satisfied?"

Alexis answered, "It's fake. I see a seam running down one side."

"I assure you, it's quite real."

"May I open the jar to test that?"

Blackburn stepped between Alexis and the jar. "To do so would risk spoiling the preservation. I can't permit it."

Alexis felt her face flushing. She didn't like it when others thought they could fool her, because she was a woman, because she was young, because she couldn't possibly be smart enough to see through their sideshow act. "Mrs. Blackburn, I don't even need to be a scientist to tell you that's a costume piece made of rubber. It's just a two-bit piece of fakery. Did you really think I wouldn't know?"

Blackburn frowned, her eyes fell into shadow, and for a second Alexis thought she saw real madness in the woman. "I'll have you know that piece was good enough for Carl Laemmle, Jr. He wants to make a movie at Universal called *The Lizard People.* He says it'll be the first talking horror picture."

A bitter laugh burst from Alexis. "One con artist duping another. Pathetic." She turned to go, but Blackburn stood between her and the heavy door, blocking her way out. "Mrs. Blackburn, I'm leaving."

Mrs. Blackburn smiled, but this one wasn't for the marks – it was the smile she kept only for the ones she couldn't fool or intimidate. In that expression, Alexis knew: May Otis Blackburn was dangerous.

"Oh, my dear," the older woman said, waving the lantern, "you will leave only when I, the prophet of The Divine Order of the Royal Arm of the Great Eleven, allow you to leave. If I were you, I'd be offering up a prayer to Michael right now."

Blackburn extinguished the lantern.

Panic caused Alexis to throw out the hand not clutching her bag, turning, reaching out. As her searching fingers found a wall and she inched forward, Blackburn erupted into laughter behind her. Alexis realized she didn't know what the other woman might have – did her pockets hold a gun? Was there an ice pick in this chamber? Perhaps an axe, used by workmen to split the blocks? Was she lifting it even now, raising it overhead as Alexis fumbled in the cold dark, reaching for –

The door. She had the handle. She yanked it, and was flooded with relief as light and hot air hit her. She didn't pause to look back, nor did she return through the house. Instead she strode around the side, to the front, in through the door, where she spotted Shufelt lounging in a chair, reading through some handwritten papers.

"We're leaving," she said.

When he just stared at her in confusion, she added, "NOW."

Shufelt dropped the papers and rose. "Let me just say goodbye –"

"No!" Alexis's shout caused Shufelt to freeze. She added, trying to sound as forceful as possible, *"we're going."*

Shufelt shrugged and led the way to the car. Once they were inside and the engine started, Alexis risked a look back. Blackburn stood on the front steps of the house – pointing at her.

"Drive!"

Shufelt threw the car into gear. Alexis felt her heart's rhythm begin to slow as they left the house behind. "Don't suppose you want to tell me what happened back there…"

Alexis hugged her bag to herself, shaking her head. "No, Warren, I don't suppose I do."

"WHAT WERE YOU LOOKING AT?" ALEXIS ASKED AS THEY WOUND THEIR way through the Santa Susana Mountains, heading back to the Valley. "The papers you were reading when we left that house?"

Shufelt tensed. "Prophecies."

Fairy tales, Alexis thought…then realized she now believed in the existence of sentient, man-sized lizards.

Outside the car, the sun had set, plunging the wild oak groves and rock outcroppings lining the road into deep shadow. The moon had just risen to their left, painting the narrow, twisting road in swaths of bluish light. Alexis rolled down her window, enjoying a rare cool wind that carried the scent of oak leaves and jasmine blossoms. On any other evening, she would have taken a moment to enjoy it - to look up to the heavens and wonder what unexplained wonders might be found beyond this small world.

But tonight was not any other evening. A cult leader had just told her that her city was controlled by angry lizard men. What if Blackburn was right, and Mulholland's terrible error had awakened something that had slept for centuries? Was there any proof? Should she tell anyone, maybe the papers? Wouldn't she be putting herself in danger?

Wasn't she already *in* danger?

The car began to slow. Alexis looked away from the side of the road to Shufelt. "Is something wrong?"

"I…heard something. Hang on while I check." Shufelt opened his door and climbed out, but stopped to look back at her. "Just stay in the car."

He disappeared.

Alexis turned, saw him walk behind the car but lost sight of him after that.

Something is very wrong. She'd never trusted Shufelt. There was nothing wrong with the car, no reason to stop it.

"Just stay in the car."

No.

She opened her door, still holding the bag in one hand, got out, walked to the rear of the car. In the red glow of the taillights, Shufelt was nowhere to be seen. "Warren?" she called out.

No response.

The entire area seemed lit with a surreal silvery moonlight, causing everything to appear painted and metallic.

Nothing felt right. *It's like someone's following me. This whole thing is spooky. But don't play into it. This is just your emotions. There's nothing to be afraid of. Shufelt left the keys in the car, so if he doesn't turn up I'll go without him -*

Something moved in the oak trees.

"What are you doing, Warren?"

No one answered, but something was definitely there, moving from tree to tree, advancing cautiously until it reached the side of the road.

Its actions unnerving and quick, the figure closed the gap between them with what felt like a blink.

Every cell in her body recoiled.

I know this.

The man stood only a few feet from her, except what she was looking at was not a man — and was not human.

Its face was long with pointed features. The eyes were larger than a human's by double, and with each blink, lids met from side to side. She recognized the movement as reptilian.

The nose was where a person's would be, only it was hill-shaped, and had nostrils ringed red. Its mouth opened, and the double-row of teeth glistened, their sharp points intimidating.

Alexis wanted to yell for Warren, but she sensed yelling might agitate the creature.

I don't have anything on me I could use to defend myself.

She put up her hands, palms out, at her waist. "Don't..." she said, but broke off, realizing there was no point in saying anything more; whatever else this thing could do, understanding English was unlikely to be among its gifts.

Alexis stood back.

As soon as she did, the creature stepped forward, matching her move.

The creature . . . the lizard . . . had the markings of a female. Alexis recognized the head shape as being round whereas a male's would be longer and thinner.

Somehow I know it's a female. I hope that means it's merciful.

She walked back again, and then again, as fast as she could, holding her bag close.

The creature matched her, move to move. There was no way she could outrun the thing.

The skin...small scales...just like the specimen. It's not a costume. It's not a fake. This is real.

Behind the lizard-thing, three smaller upright figures emerged from the shadows. Appearing more lizard than human, the children watched, their eyes bright in the night. Their arms and their claws and their tales outsized their bodies. *They look like toddlers about to be fed.*

The mother saw Alexis size up her children and rolled her head back so that her mouth was open. Sounds like clicking and low chirps came out of her in rapid waves. Her reptilian, forked tongue shot outward and flickered.

Alexis raised her free left hand up to her shoulders, showing the adult her palms. "I'm not a threat," she said. "I'm trying to help."

The lizard-thing raised her left arm, and on its end the claws curled, ready to strike.

Alexis hollered and made to duck, but the claw crashed down on her right shoulder. Her bag dropped and she fell. Pulling herself up, she noticed the claw was a different shade of dark green and grey from the rest of the lizard.

Lighter.

Younger.

That hand had been regrown.

Crouched there beneath the trees, Alexis sensed the children in front of her. They lingered and then inched closer, curious.

Their claws twitched. Their mouths opened and shut, the tips of their tongues escaping their lips, tasting the air...tasting her.

Alexis rose slowly, cautiously, just as the children closed in. One jumped on her left leg, its pointed claws digging into her like those of a kneading cat. Alexis let out a low sound, but bit back on the pain. *Don't scream. Don't hit it. They'll rip you apart.*

A chorus of sound filled the night. Chirps and clicks and strange, guttural howls. Lizard people surrounded Alexis. Their eyes seemed lit from behind, or like stars against a dark sky.

The children, hearing the chorus, retreated, running mostly on all fours, more lizard than human.

Alexis rubbed her leg where the lizard had slightly punctured her with its claw.

No longer distracted, she raised her head to see the mother still only several feet away. She had opened Alexis's bag and was staring at the photos of the hand.

Her hand.

She blinked her reptilian eyes several more times, and Alexis was sure she was a moment from being killed. *I took a hand and it wants me to pay for stealing it.*

Alexis shut her eyes as the lizard mother once more rolled back her head, joining in on the chorus — *the war cry!* — and clicked her tongue.

Please God. Please God. Make it quick. Make it quick.

She squeezed her eyes shut, and saw:

Her father showing her how to milk a cow. Collecting minnows in a pond and taking them home to watch them change into frogs.

Her childhood spent in curiosity and joy. The promise her father made that she'd be something special. It'd all be lost in a violent blink.

"I'm sorry. I didn't know. I was just trying to help," she said. She tried to keep strong. *I'm not going to go out weak, Dad. I promise you that.*

The chorus stopped.

She waited a moment, then opened her eyes a sliver, just in time to see the last shadows of the lizard people disappear as quickly as they'd come.

Rising from the ground, sure her good fortune could run out, Alexis ignored her shaking legs to make her way back to the car. Shufelt was nowhere to be found. Her gut told her she'd never see him again, that he wouldn't be returning to his teaching position at UCP.

Once she was safely back in the car, she closed the doors and window, then put her hand to the small puncture on her leg. The child had managed to get her good. The wound burned. She felt feverish and hoped she'd be able to drive back to her boarding house, where she could treat the injury. She wanted to sleep. She wanted to wake up tomorrow without a puncture wound in her leg made by an inhuman child's claw. She wanted to go back to teaching biology to young people eager to learn.

She started Shufelt's car and drove into the night.

ALEXIS AWOKE IN HER ROOM THE NEXT MORNING, ALIVE BUT NOT WELL. She called in sick, rebandaged her leg, and fell asleep.

When she woke later in the day, the fever had passed and she felt weak but knew she'd recover. She dressed, found her own car, and drove downtown.

It was 4 pm when she parked near the alley that led to Club Intime. The sun was still out, and the alley was empty at this early time of day. She found what she thought were the right steps leading down, knocked on the door at the bottom of the flight, and after a few seconds the slide was pulled back, wary eyes peering out. "Yeah?" grunted a man's voice.

"I need to see Tex. It's urgent."

The slide slammed shut.

Alexis waited, not sure if her request would be honored or not. She was still shaky from the bite, wished she was home in bed…but this had to be done. For Ambrose. For herself. For Los Angeles.

A minute later, the door opened.

She stepped into the hallway beyond as the big man with the scarred face, jacket removed and shirtsleeves pushed up, eyed her. "Don't I know you?" he asked.

"You took something from me a few nights ago."

Recognition crossed his features, then something like…concern. His voice was soft when he spoke again. "You shouldn't be here."

"I know, but…I've got nothing else."

He shrugged, led the way to the club.

Tex sat at a table in the center of the empty floor, going over a stack of receipts. She barely looked up as the beef entered with Alexis, then walked out. "Yeah? Max said you had somethin' urgent?"

Now she did look up at Alexis, and it took her a few seconds to place her. "Oh, it's you, the girl looking down the wrong hallway the other night. Didn't anyone ever tell you about curiosity and cats?"

"I know," Alexis began. "I know about the lizard people. I know about how the flood woke them up. They just killed a friend of mine and they hurt me, so at this point I'm a little desperate. I just need a few answers and I'll be on my way."

Tex pushed the receipts away to look up at Alexis. "What makes you think I know anything about this?"

"Because they're right underneath us, and you've got a door that I'm betting leads to stairs going straight down, and I saw one of them in your club the other night."

Alexis saw the woman debate with herself for a moment before she rose. "Follow me," Tex said.

Silently, she went down the hallway to the door marked "NO ADMITTANCE." Reaching into a pocket, she withdrew a key chain, fingered through it, found the right key, unlocked the door. She motioned Alexis through, and then pulled the door closed behind them, making sure it was locked. They stood together in total, subterranean darkness for a second until a light flared into Alexis's eyes, momentarily blinding her as Tex held up candlelit lantern. "This way," Tex said, moving around her to a flight of ancient wood steps. "Be careful – these things can get slippery."

Alexis followed Tex down until the stairs spilled into a tunnel carved directly into the rock beneath L.A. Barrels of liquor were stacked up against the rough walls, the floor underneath was treacherous with moisture. Tex wound through the barrels, and they proceeded this way for what Alexis guessed must be several blocks.

They were probably directly beneath the library now.

Alexis saw light ahead, realized the tunnel opened into a larger room. They reached it and Tex blocked the way for a second. "I've got a problem here you all need to deal with," she said to someone in the room. "This one's way above my pay grade."

She turned then and pushed past Alexis, making her way back. "Good luck, kid," she said in a hushed tone before disappearing down the tunnel's dark length.

Squinting against a harsh light, Alexis stepped out of the tunnel and saw what was dazzling her: the walls of this large room, the size of Tex's speakeasy, were lined in gold. In the center of the room was an elegant mahogany table, long enough to hold a sizable dinner party. All but two of the chairs around the table were empty.

The other two were occupied by William Mulholland and Aimee Semple McPherson. They looked up as Alexis stumbled in, half-blinded by all the wealth before her.

Mulholland recognized her and stood. "Miss Crawford," he called out, "you've been something of a thorn in our side."

Alexis was peering at the nearest wall, having realized that the gold was covered in a bas-relief frieze. She saw images of upright lizards on the land above, before there were even native huts; they hunted, gathered, taught their young. Another panel showed them battling men armed with primitive spears, causing them to retreat into passageways leading into the earth.

Another showed them slaying bound human captives.

Alexis turned to face the two luminaries behind her. "What is this?" she asked, indicating the story told in the gold walls.

"This," Mulholland said, "is a sort of lobby for their kingdom, which lies still further beneath."

"And why are you both here?"

Mulholland and McPherson exchanged a quick look before Sister Aimee rose, crossed to Alexis, put a firm hand on her arm, and guided her to one of the chairs around the table. "Please, dear, sit. I know how fatigued you must be, given what you've been through recently."

Alexis let herself be seated; she *was* exhausted. "So you know everything?" she asked, looking up at Mulholland and Sister Aimee as they were also seated.

"We know enough," Mulholland said.

"Did you have Ambrose killed?" she asked.

Sister Aimee leaned forward earnestly. "Oh my goodness, dear girl, no...*no*. We tried to protect him, just as we've tried to protect you."

Outrage rushed through Alexis, leaving her shaking as she said, "*Protect* me? At what point did you try to protect me – was it when a crazy woman chased me in a dark shed, or a horde of lizard people nearly killed me on a deserted hillside?"

Mulholland said, "But they didn't, did they?"

Alexis gulped, her righteousness staunched. "Why didn't they?"

"Because," he answered, "we convinced them that you might be more valuable alive than dead. They didn't recognize you until they found the photographs, then they retreated."

"What about Shufelt?"

Sister Aimee openly scoffed. "Shufelt's an idiot, just as May Otis Blackburn is. They've somehow stumbled on information they don't even know what to do with. Mrs. Blackburn will be dealt with soon enough; Shufelt is not a concern."

"And," Alexis asked, finally, the question she could no longer put off, "why am *I* important?"

Another glance between Sister Aimee and Mulholland before she said, "Why don't you take this one, William?"

He frowned, rose, paced as he walked. "You see, Miss Crawford, our reptilian friends haven't all slept over the last 500 years. Some have emerged from the underground to interact with humans; they can obviously offer great wealth –" he waved at the gold panels lining the room, "- and power. For the last hundred years, they've lived in a kind of uneasy symbiosis with us, helping some of us advance as long as we looked after their interests as well…which mainly consisted of letting them stay hidden and continuing to sleep."

"Then…well, you know what happened. It was…my fault." Mullholland turned away, and Alexis realized he was genuinely guilt-stricken over the failure of the dam.

"William," Sister Aimee said, "it's not truly your fault. *They* gave you the design for the dam, after all."

"But I should've seen it," he mumbled.

As he tried to collect himself, Alexis turned to Sister Aimee. "And you? You've worked with them, too?"

Smiling sadly, Aimee said, "That so-called kidnapping two years ago, when everyone thinks I was abducted and taken to Mexico for a month? I was actually with them, in their city beneath here."

Alexis gaped. "They have a *city*?"

"Oh yes. I suppose you could think of it as a city of devils beneath a city of angels, but…they're not really devils. They're just more of God's creations, trying to find a way ahead. When the dam broke, thousands of them died. We've spent the last week trying to convince them that it was terrible accident, even while we were trying to protect them by collecting all the…well, the parts, like the hand you found. William and I have allies among them who we're trying to convince, to avert a war."

"So," Alexis said, "now you kill me to placate them, is that it? Or you have *them* kill me, like they did Ambrose."

"Oh, no, no," Mulholland said, spinning to face her. "That's not at all why you're here, Miss Crawford."

Surprised, Alexis looked from one to the other of them, trying to find words, to frame the final question. "Then…why…?"

"Because," Sister said, walking to her, sitting beside her, taking one of her hands, "they recognize something *great* in you, as they did in William and I, and others. They want to work with you, to help you realize the dreams that you'll never find wasting your talents teaching at a backwater school."

Mulholland strode across the chamber to a great set of double doors carved in dark wood, framed by an ornate gold archway. "These doors open on the path that leads down to their city. Step through here, and your life will begin again."

"And if I don't?"

Sister Aimee said, "You're free to leave, provided that you never speak a word of this to anyone. If you do…*they'll know.*"

Her eyes darted to the darkest corners of the cavernous chamber, where Alexis saw yellow eyes blinking in the shadows.

The threat was clear.

Alexis pushed back her chair, holding herself up by gripping the edge of the table, her legs numb. "So my choice is to make a deal with them and become famous, or leave and never say a word to anyone."

Mulholland nodded. Sister Aimee gazed at her hopefully.

Alexis didn't need long to make the decision.

THE SUN WAS SETTING AS SHE DROVE BACK TO HER BOARDING HOUSE. She wanted to crawl back into bed, sleep for twelve hours, and try to go back to the school tomorrow. She'd return the gold figurine to the student who had loaned it to her, advise him to melt it down for the precious metal. Perhaps there'd be a message from her insurance company, giving her a check to help with rebuilding her home.

But she knew the world would never be the same. She'd seen deception, and the black heart beneath. Los Angeles lay spread below a bright sun, but its secrets belonged to the darkest night. Those secrets would stay with her as long as she lived, which she hoped would be long enough to realize some of her dreams on her own.

THE END

CEMETERY DANCE
PUBLICATIONS

We hope you enjoyed your
Cemetery Dance Paperback!
Share pictures of them online, and tag us!

Instagram: @cemeterydancepub
Twitter: @CemeteryEbook
TikTok: @cemeterydancepub
www.facebook.com/CDebookpaperbacks

Use the following tags!

#horrorbook #horror #horrorbooks
#bookstagram #horrorbookstagram
#horrorpaperbacks #horrorreads
#bookstagrammer #horrorcommunity
#cemeterydancepublications

SHARE THE HORROR!

Cemetery Dance Publications Paperbacks and Ebooks!

BAD MOON RISING
by Luisa Colon

In Gravesend, Brooklyn, sixteen-year-old Elodia is an outcast at school, at odds with her father, and longing for her mysteriously absent mother. Lonely and isolated, Elodia knows that something unspeakably terrible has happened to her—she just can't remember what....

"Twisty and disturbing, Bad Moon Rising is an ambitious, moody meditation on the cycles of familial trauma. Luisa Colon's impressive debut is sure to get under your skin."
—Paul Tremblay, author of *The Cabin at the End of the World*

SMOKE, IN CRIMSON,
by Greg F. Gifune

Haunted by his dark past and an array of addictions that destroyed his life, Deacon is a man adrift, a lost soul trying to piece back together all that's been lost....

"A daring, claustrophobic bit of dark art about the pull of obsession and the monsters who take strength from our weaknesses. Equal parts haunting, sad, and darkly beautiful, this is Gifune in top form."
—Ronald Malfi, author of *Black Mouth*

THE NIGHT PROPHETS,
by Paul F. Olson

Universal Ministries was the fastest growing religious group in the country, but Curt Potter joined it to meet his father, Reverend Arthur Bach, the charismatic founder of the church. But Curt and his fellow initiates make a shocking discovery:
That the church hides a dark, horribly secret...

"If you are looking for an action packed, blood soaked, character driven tale that just happens to be a vampire story, you need look no further than The Night Prophets. Enjoyed every minute of it."
—Literary Mayhem

Purchase these and other fine works of horror from Cemetery Dance Publications today!

https://www.cemeterydance.com/

HORROR
DNA
MOVIES
COMIC BOOKS
MUSIC
BOOKS
VIDEO GAMES
IT'S IN
OUR
BLOOD
horrordna.com